DISCARD

j940.54   Hamilton, John
HAM

World War II:
The final years

CHILDREN'S ROOM

MAR 2 2 2012   839

FAIRPORT PUBLIC LIBRARY
1 Village Landing
Fairport, NY 14450

WORLD WAR II
THE FINAL YEARS

BY JOHN HAMILTON

VISIT US AT
WWW.ABDOPUBLISHING.COM

Published by ABDO Publishing Company, 8000 West 78th Street, Suite 310, Edina, MN 55439. Copyright ©2012 by Abdo Consulting Group, Inc. International copyrights reserved in all countries. No part of this book may be reproduced in any form without written permission from the publisher. ABDO & Daughters™ is a trademark and logo of ABDO Publishing Company.

Printed in the United States of America, North Mankato, Minnesota.
082011
092011

 PRINTED ON RECYCLED PAPER

Editor: Sue Hamilton
Graphic Design: John Hamilton
Cover Design: Neil Klinepier
Cover Photo: National Archives and Records Administration (NARA)
Interior Photos and Illustrations: AP-pgs 20-21, 23 (bottom), 25 & 26; Black Archives of Mid-America in Kansas City-pg 6 (top); Corbis-pgs 15 (inset) & 18-19; Digital Stock-pgs 14-15; Getty Images-pgs 8-13, 23 (top) & 28; Granger Collection-pgs 22 & 27; Hiroshima Peace Memorial Museum-pg 27 (top); John Hamilton-maps on pgs 9, 14 & 20; Library of Congress-pgs 4-5 & 7; Margaret Bourke-White-pg 17 (inset); NARA-pgs 1, 3, 8 (inset), 19 (inset), 24 & 29; National Museum of American History-pg 6 (poster inset); U.S. Air Force-pg 27 (inset); US Holocaust Memorial Museum-pgs 16-17.

ABDO Booklinks
To learn more about World War II, visit ABDO Publishing Company online. Web sites about World War II are featured on our Book Links pages. These links are routinely monitored and updated to provide the most current information available. Web site: www.abdopublishing.com

Library of Congress Cataloging-in-Publication Data

Hamilton, John, 1959-
　World War II : the final years / John Hamilton.
　　　p. cm. -- (World War II)
　Includes index.
　ISBN 978-1-61783-060-0
　1. World War, 1939-1945--Juvenile literature. I. Title.
D743.7.H365 2012
940.53--dc23
　　　　　　　　　　2011020132

CONTENTS

The War at Home 4

The Liberation of France 8

Operation Market Garden 10

The Battle of the Bulge 12

The Holocaust 16

The Fall of Berlin 18

Victory in the Pacific 20

The Defeat of Japan 26

The Aftermath 28

Glossary 30

Index 32

A soldier stands guard on a lonely beach.

THE WAR AT HOME

World War II brought great suffering to many people around the world. Millions of soldiers and civilians were killed or starved to death, and entire cities were reduced to rubble. But in the United States, the economy improved. Almost every factory in the land converted to producing goods for the military, including airplanes, ships, bombs, and trucks.

Just weeks after the attack by Japan on the U.S. naval base at Pearl Harbor, Hawaii, President Franklin D. Roosevelt urged everyone in the country to help the war effort: "We must have more ships, more guns, more planes—more of everything. We must be the great arsenal of democracy." During the Great Depression, one out of every four workers was unemployed. During World War II, the unemployment rate dipped down to about one percent, a record low.

From 1940 to 1945, many consumer items were scarce or simply not for sale. Other goods had to be rationed. People received ration coupons they could use to buy scarce items like meat, sugar, and coffee. Gasoline and rubber goods were also rationed.

Because so many were now employed, and there were so few goods to buy, many people invested their money in war bonds. The U.S. government used this borrowed money to pay for the cost of the war.

Workers at Willow Run manufacturing plant in Ypsilanti, Michigan, install a motor on a B-24 Liberator bomber in the 1940s.

The Tuskegee Airmen were African American combat pilots in World War II.

During World War II, many parts of American society changed. Millions of soldiers went off to fight overseas, leaving jobs open in the nation's bustling factories. Many women filled these jobs. They did work that was previously reserved for men, such as riveting and welding. The image of "Rosie the Riveter"  represented a first taste of equal rights for American women. African Americans, too, found well-paying factory jobs. Many migrated from poverty stricken areas of the Deep South to take jobs in other places, such as the West Coast or the Midwest.

Racism and sexism, however, remained in American society. Women who joined the armed forces held only support jobs, although combat nurses were often in danger near the front lines. African Americans in the military were at first segregated and given jobs such as truck drivers or cooks. Gradually, African Americans played a bigger fighting role in the war. The Tuskegee Airmen were a group of African American combat pilots who shot down many Nazis over the skies of Europe.

After Pearl Harbor, some Americans were concerned about the loyalty of Japanese people living in this country. Thousands of Japanese Americans were forced to leave their homes and move to war relocation camps, such as Manzanar in California.

Many ethnic groups were discriminated against during the war. Japanese Americans suffered especially hard. After the Pearl Harbor attack, anti-Japanese hysteria swept the nation. People were afraid some Japanese Americans might be spies for Japan. About 110,000 Japanese Americans were sent to internment camps in remote areas, prisoners of their own government, until the beginning of 1945.

The LIBERATION OF FRANCE

After the successful D-Day invasion in June 1944, the next step for the Allies was to break out of Normandy in northern France and liberate the rest of the country. The Germans didn't make this an easy task, putting up fierce resistance every step of the way. Pressing forward was also difficult because of the French countryside, which included thick hedgerows, forests, and shallow trenches.

After two months of fighting, Allied armor finally broke through the German lines. Led by General George Patton, the U.S. Third Army raced across France, pushing enemy forces back across Belgium and toward the German border. Sometimes Patton's tanks moved so far ahead that they outran their fuel supplies. By the end of August, the French capital of Paris was liberated.

Also in August, the Allies landed a second invasion force in southern France. They pushed northwards, increasing the pressure on the Germans. Soon, the enemy was on the run. With France mostly liberated, the next step for the Allies was to invade Germany itself.

An Allied victory parade in Paris, France, on August 29, 1944.

JUNE–DECEMBER 1944

American soldiers taking cover in a ditch during the invasion of Normandy, France.

By December 1944, the Allies had pushed German forces almost completely out of France.

9

OPERATION MARKET GARDEN

As the autumn of 1944 approached, the Allies hoped they could invade Germany by Christmas and put an end to the war in Europe. But as the military advanced through France, their supply lines grew thin. Gasoline, food, and other critical goods became more and more difficult to send to the front lines.

British Field Marshal Bernard Montgomery devised a plan to invade Germany from the north, through the Nazi-occupied Netherlands. He convinced General Dwight Eisenhower, Supreme Commander of Allied forces in Europe, to go ahead with the plan, despite objections from other American commanders.

Operation Market Garden was launched in mid-September 1944. About 42,000 British and American airborne troops parachuted into the Netherlands. It was the largest airborne operation of the war. Their mission was to capture a series of bridges over critical river crossings. This would allow Allied forces to slip into northern Germany and then push to the capital of Berlin, hopefully ending the war.

The Allied troops met heavier-than-expected Nazi resistance, including powerful *panzers* (tanks). The last bridge over the Lower Rhine River, at the city of Arnhem, was not taken. It was "a bridge too far." The Allies suffered thousands of casualties, and were forced to abandon the operation.

Allied Sherman tanks crossing a bridge at Nijmegen in Holland during their advance as part of Operation Market Garden in September 1944.

Waves of airborne troops parachute into the Netherlands during Operation Market Garden.

SEPTEMBER 1944

The BATTLE OF THE BULGE

With the German army's losses stacking up, Adolf Hitler decided to try something drastic. Instead of defending the German border, he wanted to launch a surprise attack on the Allies. Using the same *blitzkrieg* tactics that had proven so effective in the early years of the war, he wanted to smash through the Allied forces, encircle them, and cripple them. He hoped this would force the Allies to withdraw, or negotiate a cease fire. It was Hitler's last chance to win the war.

On December 16, 1944, fresh columns of German *panzers* (tanks) pushed through Belgium's forested mountain region called the Ardennes. American forces in the area were caught by surprise. Bad weather prevented air support. The battle resulted in some of the heaviest fighting of the war. About 19,000 Americans were killed, and almost 70,000 wounded or captured. For a time, it seemed that the Germans might actually win.

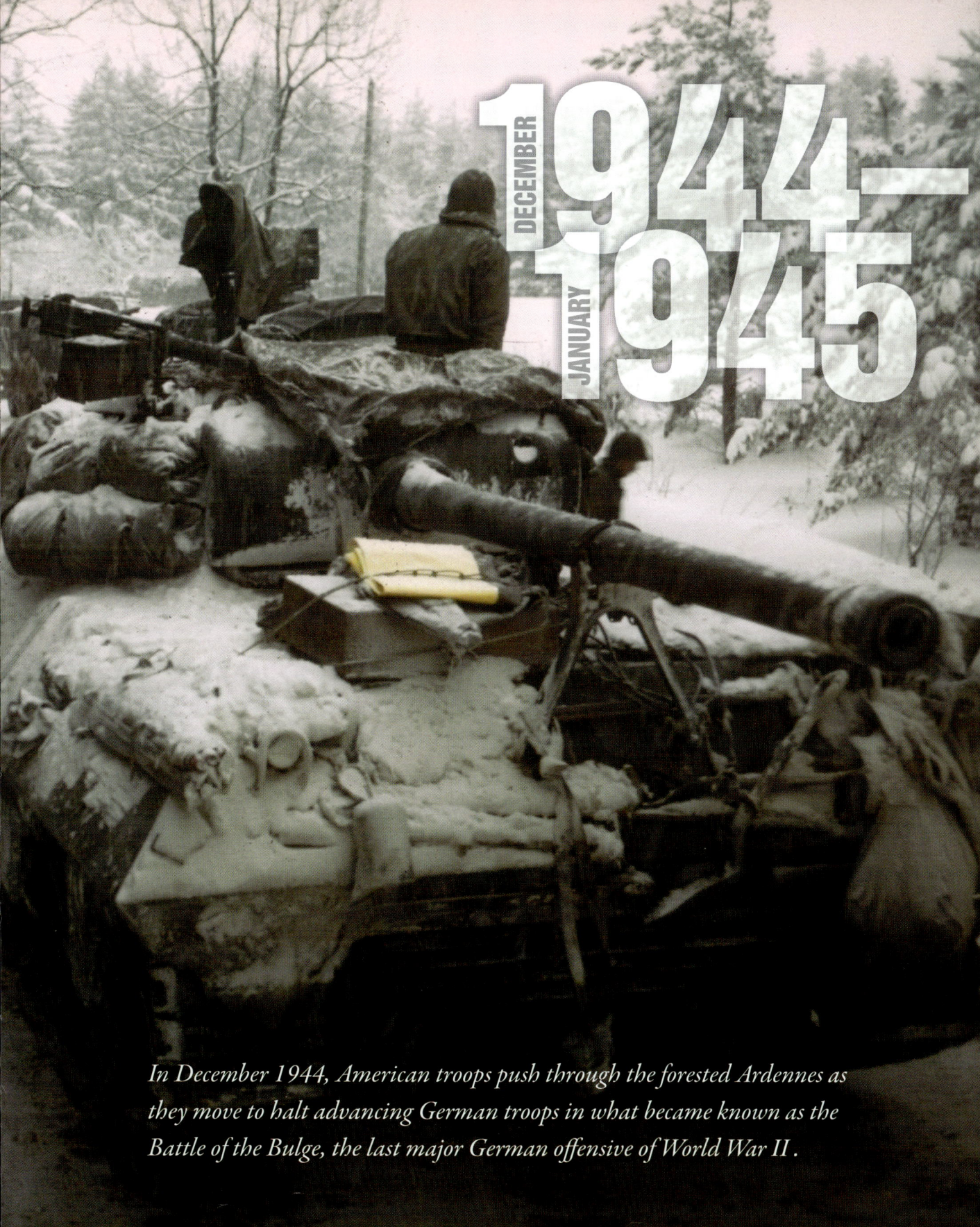

DECEMBER 1944– JANUARY 1945

In December 1944, American troops push through the forested Ardennes as they move to halt advancing German troops in what became known as the Battle of the Bulge, the last major German offensive of World War II.

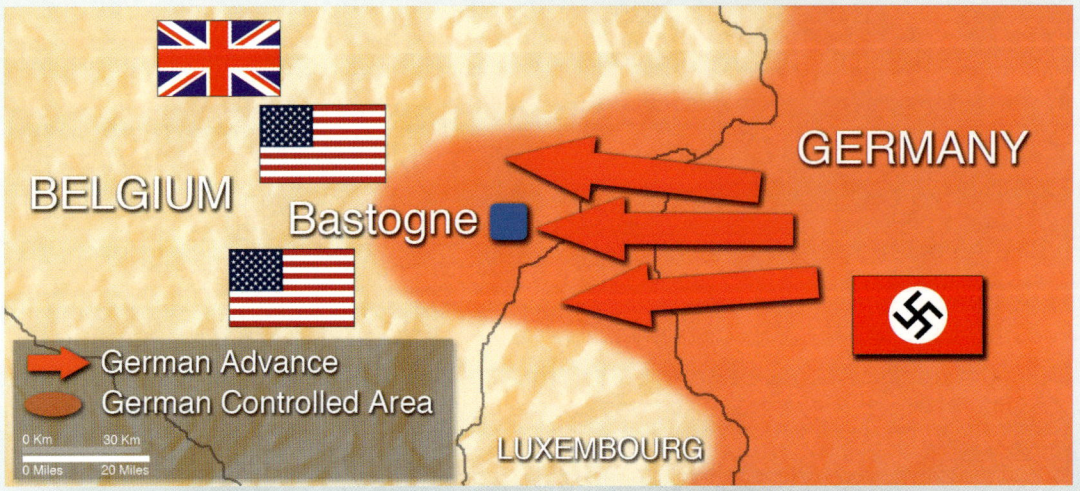

The Battle of the Bulge is named after the shape of how the German attack looks on a map. In military terms, it is called a "salient."

Winter fighting in the rugged Ardennes was miserable. Thousands were injured because of the cold, and food was scarce. Combat was savage, a desperate fight for survival. For the Americans, it would prove to be the bloodiest battle of the war.

Despite being outnumbered and out-equipped, the Americans fought bravely. In the besieged Belgium town of Bastogne, General Anthony McAuliffe was asked by the Nazis if he wished to surrender. His response: "Nuts!" The Americans fought on.

By December 23, the weather improved. Allied planes began attacking German tanks and troops. American and British soldiers finally received supplies such as food, ammunition, and gasoline.

The Germans received no such resupplies, and soon their tanks began running out of gas. By December 24, the German advance had stalled.

On December 26, General George Patton's Third Army arrived at Bastogne, ending the siege. By the end of January 1945, the Nazi offensive had been crushed, most of their tanks destroyed, and the enemy sent fleeing back to Germany.

After some of the deadliest fighting of the war, American troops began retaking the area around Bastogne. Many German soldiers were killed or taken prisoner.

Infantrymen advance across an open, snowy field during the Battle of the Bulge.

15

THE HOLOCAUST

In April 1945, when American troops entered the Buchenwald prison camp near Weimar, Germany, they were shocked at what they discovered. Thousands of gaunt, malnourished prisoners greeted the Americans. The soldiers also found piles of corpses and mass graves.

Buchenwald was one of many "concentration" camps built in Germany and Poland. Adolf Hitler wanted to exterminate all Jews in German-controlled areas. He blamed Jewish people for many of Germany's problems. The Nazi SS secret police removed Jews from their homes and sent them to the camps.

Some camps, such as Auschwitz in Poland, were built solely to exterminate prisoners. They were called death camps. In other camps, many Jews were put to work as slave laborers in German factories. They were mistreated and poorly fed. When they were too weak to work, they were executed.

Jewish people are rounded up in Warsaw, Poland.

By the end of World War II, nearly two out of three European Jews were killed, about six million people. Approximately 1.5 million victims were children. This period of Nazi murder of the Jewish people is today called the Holocaust.

The FALL OF BERLIN

By the end of January 1945, the war situation for Germany was hopeless. And yet Hitler fought on. The Allies responded with relentless air attacks on German cities. Historic Dresden was bombed and reduced to rubble in February, killing an estimated 25,000 civilians.

In April, the Allies launched ground offenses against Germany. American forces attacked from the west, while Soviet troops invaded from the east. They linked up at the Elbe River on April 25, 1945.

The Allies agreed that Soviet Union troops would attack the German capital of Berlin. Fighting was savage, some of the worst of the war. The Red Army fought street-to-street, and house-to-house. By the end of the battle, most of the city was destroyed. The Soviets suffered more than 300,000 casualties. The Germans lost 100,000 soldiers.

On April 30, 1945, Soviet troops reached the city center and raised their flag over the Reichstag, the German parliament building. That same day, Adolf Hitler committed suicide. German forces began to surrender.

JANUARY–MAY 1945

May 8 was designated V-E Day, which stood for "Victory in Europe." People in Allied cities all over the world celebrated. But for soldiers in the Pacific Theater, there was still much fighting to be done.

Berlin is reduced to rubble as Soviet troops enter the city.

VICTORY IN THE PACIFIC

Less than three years after the Japanese attack on Pearl Harbor, Hawaii, the United States Navy had rebuilt and expanded its Pacific Ocean fleet. Carrier task forces included powerful aircraft carriers and other warships. United States Marines were now highly skilled at making amphibious assaults on enemy beaches.

As they fought their way toward the Japanese homeland, the Navy used an "island hopping" strategy against Japanese-controlled islands. Some enemy strongholds were simply bypassed. Islands that were leapfrogged were cut off from critical supplies such as oil and food. American submarines also preyed on Japanese cargo ships, further restricting the enemy's supplies.

1943–1945

While British and Australian forces fought the Japanese in Burma and New Guinea, the United States attacked strongholds in the Solomon, Gilbert, Marshall, and Mariana Islands. Fighting was fierce in places such as Tarawa and Saipan (shown here). Most Japanese defenders fought to the death instead of suffering the humiliation of defeat. Thousands of American troops died taking the heavily defended islands, but the Japanese lost many more soldiers. Very few were captured.

A Japanese plane goes down after being hit by American antiaircraft guns.

In June 1944, in the Battle of the Philippine Sea, Japan attacked U.S. naval forces with almost every remaining carrier-based aircraft it had left. Days earlier, American Marines and Army troops had launched an amphibious assault on Saipan in the Mariana Islands. As fighting on the island raged, the Japanese fleet moved into position. But it was no match for the Americans.

The battle was so lopsided—more than 600 Japanese planes were shot down—that the Americans called it the "Great Marianas Turkey Shoot." By this point in the war, Japan had lost its most experienced pilots, and its planes were inferior to new American aircraft such as the Grumman Hellcat fighter. The Japanese Imperial Navy also lost three aircraft carriers in the battle.

A Grumman Hellcat fighter.

In October 1944, the Japanese made one last try to destroy the American fleet as U.S. troops invaded the Philippine island of Leyte. The Battle of Leyte Gulf was the largest naval battle of World War II. The Americans lost six warships and 3,500 men. For the Japanese, the battle was a complete disaster. The Imperial Navy lost 27 warships and more than 10,000 men.

By this point in the war, about 90 percent of Japan's ships had been sunk or severely damaged. Japanese sea power could no longer stop the American Navy.

At the Battle of Leyte Gulf, some Japanese pilots crashed their planes into U.S. warships. These suicide bombers were called *kamikaze*, a Japanese word meaning "divine wind."

23

Marines raise the American flag on the island of Iwo Jima in February 1945.

On February 19, 1945, United States Marines stormed ashore on a small volcanic island called Iwo Jima, about 750 miles (1,207 km) south of Tokyo, Japan. Taking Iwo Jima would deny the Japanese a base, and the U.S. could also use the island's airstrips to launch attacks against mainland Japan.

Japanese forces on the island were larger than expected. They fought ferociously to defend their positions, which included a network of hardened bunkers and underground tunnels.

The Americans won the battle, but it was costly for both sides. After five weeks of fighting, the Marines suffered more than 26,000 casualties. Almost all of the 22,000 Japanese defenders were killed. Only 216 were captured.

U.S. Marines on Okinawa use dynamite to seal a cave that hid Japanese soldiers.

The Americans fought another brutal battle from April to June 1945 on the island of Okinawa, which is part of Japan's Ryukyu Island chain. Only 340 miles (547 km) from the mainland, Okinawa would have made an excellent base to launch attacks on Japan.

Fighting was intense and horrifying. Stubborn Japanese soldiers in bunkers and caves were either blown up or burned out with flamethrowers. Thousands of Japanese launched themselves at the Americans in suicidal "*banzai*" charges. Kamikaze pilots crashed their planes into American ships. By the end of the battle, the Americans suffered more than 50,000 killed or wounded. The Japanese lost 70,000 soldiers. More than 150,000 civilians died.

The DEFEAT OF JAPAN

The bloody Battle of Okinawa was a chilling preview of the kind of fanatical resistance U.S. military planners expected when the time came to invade the Japanese mainland. To make the enemy as weak as possible before the invasion, U.S. B-29 Superfortress bombers carried out air raids on Japanese cities, including the capital of Tokyo. Thousands of civilians were killed.

In July 1945, American scientists successfully tested a new weapon at Los Alamos, New Mexico. The atomic bomb was the result of the Manhattan Project, a top-secret effort to unleash the energy in atoms, the small particles that make up all matter.

Hoping to bring the war to a speedy end, President Harry Truman authorized the use of atomic weapons against Japan. On August 6, 1945, the American B-29 bomber *Enola Gay* dropped an atomic bomb on the industrial city of Hiroshima. Estimates vary widely, but the death toll was at least between 70,000 to 80,000 people from this single bomb. On August 9, Nagasaki was attacked. At least another 40,000 people died.

The Japanese had little choice. Emperor Hirohito announced Japan's unconditional surrender on August 15, 1945. On September 2, formal surrender documents were signed on the battleship USS *Missouri*. World War II was over.

A B-29 Superfortress bombs a Japanese target in July 1945.

AUGUST 6, 1945
1945

An atom bomb is dropped on Hiroshima.

The *Enola Gay* returns to base after its bombing mission.

Hiroshima lies in ruins after the atomic blast.

THE AFTERMATH

After the war ended in 1945, Germany and Japan were occupied for many years by Allied soldiers. Both countries were shattered. There was little resistance to occupation. People just wanted to find a way to survive.

Germany was divided into four zones that were temporarily controlled by the United States, the United Kingdom, France, and the Soviet Union. In Japan, the occupation was run by the United States, with General Douglas MacArthur leading the effort. In both countries, war criminals were prosecuted and new governments were created. Today, both Germany and Japan are robust democracies with strong ties to the United States and other Western countries.

Between 50 and 70 million people lost their lives during the war. It took many decades for countries to rebuild and for old hostilities to fade.

Today we remember World War II as an epic struggle of good versus evil. The story of the war is retold through countless books, movies, museums, and commemorations. As the war's veterans grow ever older and fade from this Earth, it is up to younger generations to remember their sacrifice, and to make sure the world is never again plunged into a conflict like the epic tragedy of World War II.

Japan signs surrender papers aboard the USS Missouri on September 2, 1945, ending the war.

Two members of the Coast Guard salute a fallen veteran of World War II.

GLOSSARY

Allies
The Allies were the many nations that were allied, or joined, in the fight against Germany, Italy, and Japan in World War II. The most powerful nations among the Allies included the United States, Great Britain, the Soviet Union, France, China, Canada, and Australia.

Banzai
A Japanese battle cry, used in a fearless and reckless attack.

Blitzkrieg
A German word meaning "lightning warfare." It described a new strategy that the German military used in World War II. *Blitzkrieg* called for very large invasions to overwhelm the enemy quickly with combined land and air attacks in order to avoid long, drawn-out battles.

Casualty
Soldiers and civilians reported as either killed, wounded, or missing in action.

Democracy
Democracies have elected governments that protect the rights of individual citizens.

Fighter
A small, fast plane that is used to battle other planes in the air. Fighters were often used to escort large and slow bomber planes over enemy territory.

Great Depression
The Great Depression was a period of severe economic downturn, starting in 1929 and lasting about a decade. Jobs were scarce and few people had extra money.

Kamikaze

A Japanese word that means "divine wind." It refers to a period in Japanese history when two massive Mongol invasion fleets, one in 1274 and the other in 1281, were miraculously destroyed by typhoons (hurricanes). Japanese suicide pilots of World War II were called kamikaze because it was hoped they would destroy enough U.S. warships to defeat the enemy. Although terrifying, the kamikaze attacks had little overall effect.

Nazi

The Nazi Party was the political party in Germany that supported Adolf Hitler. After 1934 it was the only political party allowed in Germany. This is when Hitler became a dictator and ruled Germany with total power.

SS

A Nazi secret police organization that was originally created to be Adolf Hitler's bodyguard. The initials SS stand for the German word *schutzstaffen*, which means "protection squad." As the war progressed, the SS was placed in charge of concentration camps and the extermination of Jewish people and other persecuted groups.

Anne Frank was a young German Jew who lived in Amsterdam, in the Netherlands. She hid in a secret room for two years before being discovered by Nazis and sent to a concentration camp, where she later died. Her book, The Diary of a Young Girl, *is today read by schoolchildren the world over.*

INDEX

A
Allies 8, 10, 12, 18
Amsterdam, Netherlands 31
Ardennes Forest 12, 13, 14
army, German 12
Army, U.S. 22
Arnhem, Netherlands 10
Auschwitz 16

B
B-29 Superfortress bomber 26
banzai 25
Bastogne, Belgium 14
Belgium 8, 12, 13, 14
Berlin, Germany 10, 18, 19
blitzkrieg 12
Buchenwald 16
Bulge, Battle of the 13, 14
Burma 21

C
California 7
Christmas 10

D
D-Day 8
Deep South 6
Diary of a Young Girl, The 31
Dresden, Germany 18

E
Earth 28
Eisenhower, Dwight 10
Elbe River 18
Enola Gay (B-29 bomber) 26
Europe 6, 10

F
France 8, 10, 28
Frank, Anne 31

G
Germany 8, 10, 14, 16, 18, 28
Gilbert Islands 21
Great Depression 4
Great Marianas Turkey Shoot 22
Grumman 22

H
Hawaii 4, 20
Hellcat fighter 22
Hirohito, Emperor 26
Hiroshima, Japan 26
Hitler, Adolf 12, 16, 18
Holland 11
Holocaust 17

I
Imperial Navy, Japanese 22, 23
Iwo Jima 24

J
Japan 4, 7, 22, 23, 24, 25, 26, 28
Jews 16, 17, 31

K
kamikaze 23, 25

L
Leyte, Philippines 23
Leyte Gulf, Battle of 23
Los Alamos, NM 26
Lower Rhine River 10

M
MacArthur, Douglas 28
Manhattan Project 26
Manzanar 7
Mariana Islands 21, 22
Marines, U.S. 20, 22, 24
Marshall Islands 21
McAuliffe, Anthony 14
Midwest 6
Missouri, USS 26
Montgomery, Bernard 10

N
Nagasaki, Japan 26
Navy, U.S. 20, 22, 23
Nazis 6, 10, 14, 16, 17, 31
Netherlands 10, 31
New Guinea 21
New Mexico 26
Normandy, France 8

O
Okinawa 25
Okinawa, Battle of 26
Operation Market Garden 10, 11

P
Pacific Ocean 20
Pacific Theater 19
panzers 10, 12
Paris, France 8
Patton, George 8, 14
Pearl Harbor, Hawaii 4, 7, 20
Philippine Sea, Battle of the 22
Philippines 23
Poland 16

R
Red Army 18
Reichstag 18
Roosevelt, Franklin D. 4
Rosie the Riveter 6
Ryukyu Islands 25

S
Saipan 21, 22
salient 14
Solomon Islands 21
Soviet Union 18, 28
SS 16

T
Tarawa 21
Third Army, U.S. 8, 14
Tokyo, Japan 24, 26
Truman, Harry 26
Tuskegee Airmen 6

U
United Kingdom 28
United States 4, 21, 22, 23, 24, 26, 28

V
V-E Day 19
Victory in Europe (*see* V-E Day)

W
Weimar, Germany 16
West Coast 6